Color Friends

Written & Illustrated
by Laurie Hartsook

HartsookPress
Sebastopol, CA 95472

Story and pictures: Laurie Hartsook
Book Design & Publishing Services: Constance King Design

ISBN 978-1-7342724-0-6

Hartsook Press
Sebastopol, CA 95472
lauriehartsook@gmail.com

Dedicated to

Jude and Owen

who color my life

Part 1

When
Blue

Meets
Yellow

Once Upon a Time,

there was only

blue.

up,

down,

swirl around,

only blue.

Then one day,

BANG!

Yellow

appeared, just like
THAT!

"Who are you?" Yellow asked.

"I am Blue."
He was shy, but curious about
this new shining color.

Yellow was also curious.
"Can I touch you?"
Blue nodded.
Wherever Yellow touched blue,
a most wondrous thing happened.
A new friend appeared.

It was **Green.**

Green swirled along with Yellow.
He moved into Blue's heart.
He felt the coolness of the moon
and the warmth of the sun.

"Yellow spun into a

giant
ball

leaving trails of bright light.

Blue
and
green
moved around with her,

reaching

far

into

space.

Faster

and faster

they whirled.

Splinters of Blue

flew off

into the light.

Time slowed down. The colors blurred,

Until at last Green

emerged.

He felt peaceful like

Blue

and Brilliant like

Yellow.

"Yellow, where are you? Are you lost?" called Blue.

"I'm here but I can't see you."

Just then ...

Blue

came out of the shadows.

Green

leaped down to the Ground.

Yellow

rose to the heights.

Blue

gently surrounded

Yellow.

Together
they created Light.

Shining down

on the green ground,

they warmed the earth

and helped it grow.

Part 2

When
Yellow
Meets
Red

20

In the land of Yellow
all was bright.

The **air** itself
was infused with light.

In the center was the
sun,
with the **moon**
sitting on top.

As if by magic,

red appeared

like a belly button

inside the sun.

Red began to spiral out.

Around she went like the rim of a seashell.

"Who is that?" asked Yellow.

"An orange head
popped out where
the moon used to be,"
laughed Red.

The head cocked,
amazed at his new wings.

Yellow and Red

were creating a bird,

one so unique

that the sun smiled

Red said, "Tell me Yellow,

when it is time to mix together."

"It is time!"

Orange

dark and light,

Orange

vibrant and bright.

Now the **bird** stands up

ready to **fly**

soars across the sky.

waving his wings he

One day something told the **bird**
to make a nest of twigs and leaves.

The nest began to S M O K E,
flames flickered and a fire

sPARKED!

The **bird** fluttered his wings and
became one with the fire.

A heavy **red** cloud

filled the air

while Yellow

fanned the fallen ashes.

heavens.

the

to

rose

Smoke

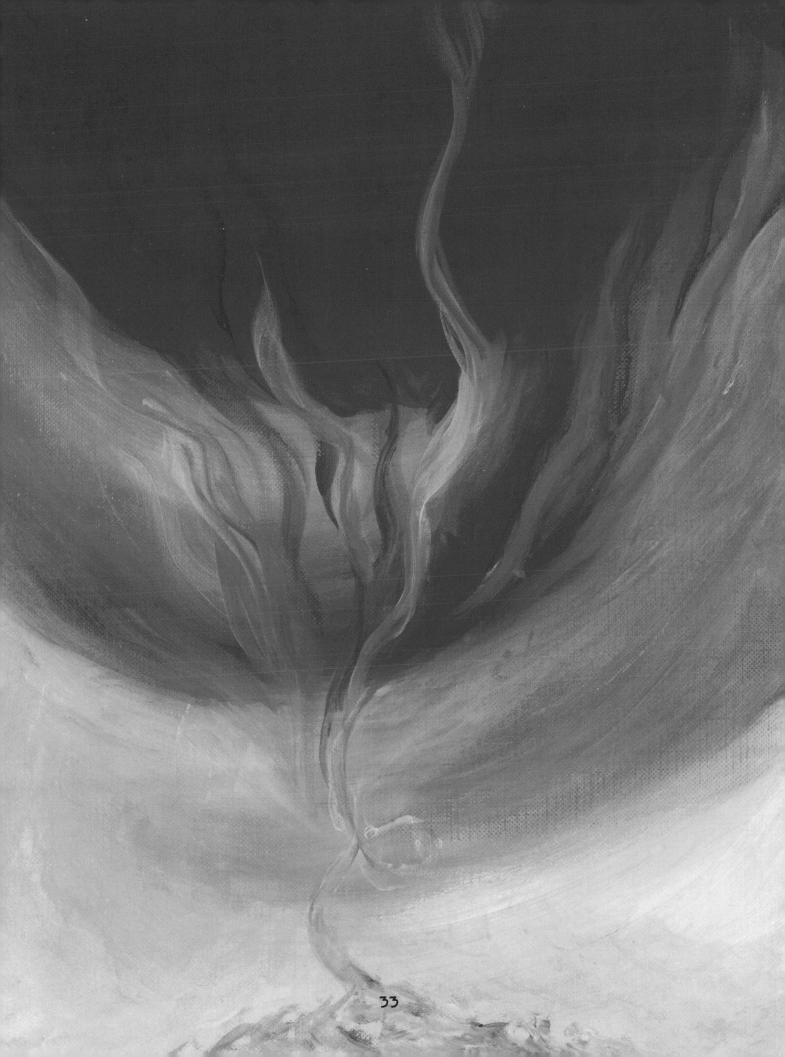

33

34

Out of the ashes
a new **bird** appeared

full of wonder,
full of delight,

a beautiful blend of
warmth and **light**.

The **bird** grew
and he flew to the **sun.**

He didn't get burned
because he was
born out of fire.

If you are very lucky
you may see one someday.
This bird is called a

Phoenix

and it is full of magic
and wonder.

— Part 3 —

when

Red

Meets

Blue

40

Red

is strong.

Red

is beautiful.

Red

believes she can do anything.

But **day** after **day**

of just Red gets boring.

"Is there anyone

to play with?"

called **Red.**

Then **Blue** came

floating

down

like

a cloud

in a

light patch

of sky.

Red said, "Good to see you **Blue.**

Phew! you are cooling me off."

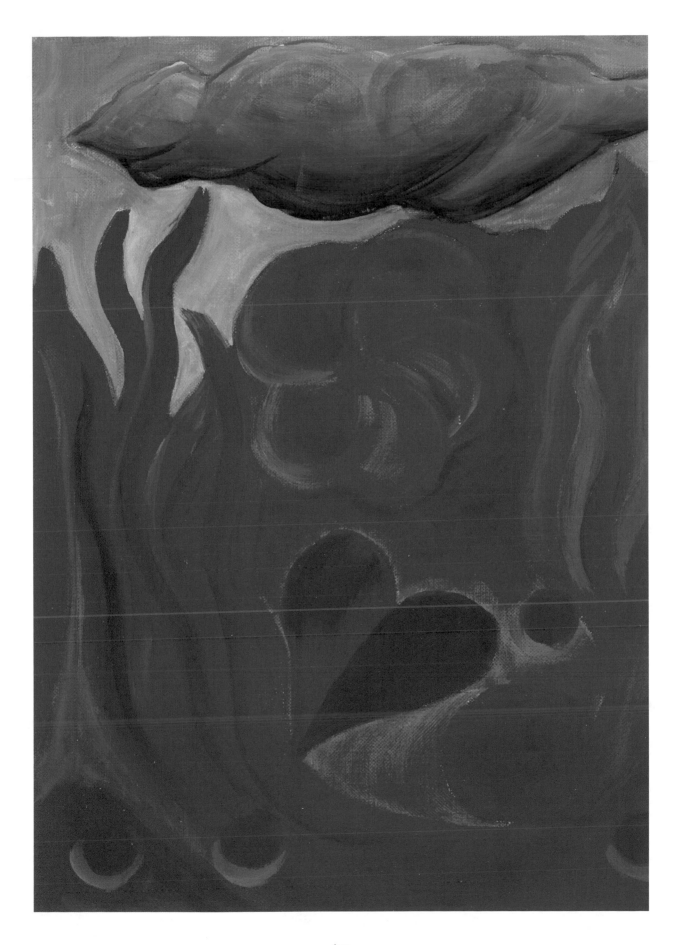

Just then a warm wind ran through
Blue.

A cool current shivered through
Red.

They glided past each other.

"Hi!" said Red.

"Bye!" said Blue.

45

They passed again.

Red became a wave and ... whoosh!

Pushed into her friend **Blue.**

Some of **Red** and some of **Blue** tumbled below, into the foamy **white.**

"I will play Red's game," thought

Blue

who snaked his way into

Red.

They tied themselves into knots.
They made ribbons of color
and magical Rings.

"Hello friends,"
said a new voice. It was

Purple.

49

Just then a HUGE WIND took the colors for a ride.

They swirled like a hurricane holding onto the eye.

They swirled until ...

white lights twinkled all around.

Blue said,

"That was a **wild** ride!

But now I feel so calm."

Purple added,

"This must be space."

"Look!"

There was **Red,** as still

as Red could be.

All the planets
were born
in the

Purple

space:

planets with
spinning rings,
a warm one,
a cool one,
a watery one,
and ones
we cannot see.

Part 4

When the
Colors
Come
Together

58

One fine spring day,
Yellow shone especially bright in the sky.
Purple created thick clouds.
Blue sent raindrops through the sunlight.

Magically all the color friends appeared!

In a rainbow spanning the sky,
Red, Orange, Yellow,
Green, Blue **and Purple**

stood side by side.

The next time you see a rainbow, can you
find all the color friends?

Notes to Parents, Teachers, and Artists of All Ages

We are surrounded by color everyday, wherever we go. Imagine a world without color, and you can appreciate how it enriches our lives. Colors affect us emotionally, whether we are conscious of it or not. Have you ever described your mood with color? Have you ever felt the blues, or has the blue sky ever left you feeling at peace? Have you ever gotten red hot mad? Red may also uplift or engage us. Imagine you are ensouled with golden yellow, or wrapped in a deep purple cloak. Paying attention to color can help people of all ages appreciate beauty and understand ourselves. Meditating on different colors can energize, balance or calm us. Color is taken in through our sense of sight, but gives us more than what the eye can perceive. Imagine a conversation with a blind person; how would you describe orange; maybe with a feeling or sensation?

Ascribing emotion to color is often helpful, especially for children. My experience working with color stems from teaching in a Waldorf School. The first grader begins painting with only one color at a time. Some children love to paint red, while others prefer blue. Some love to mix red and yellow; others love to create green. Applying Rudolf Steiner's ideas of the four temperaments and their colors, we can better understand our psychology. For example, a melancholic temperament, represented by cool blue, tends toward compassion but also sadness. The choleric, seen as red, bursts into the world with fiery passion. Phlegmatic green moves methodically, tends to be good natured but may be stubborn. Yellow, the sanguine temperament, lives with light heartedness, enjoys talking and starting projects. Just as there is no absolute red, we too are a blend of hues, and colors.

In my painting lessons, I sometimes personified the colors in stories, which brought delight to the children. They saw themselves and their classmates in the color friends. They noticed which ones harmonize and which ones compete. In this story, I brought the primary colors, and they showed me what they wanted to create together. The abstract style leaves much to the imagination. In my personification, red is she and blue is he, however it could just as naturally be the opposite. Every gender may live in every color. I hope you are inspired to paint, and explore color in the world. Thank you Ruby and Lisa for asking for more color! May we all embrace the full rainbow of life.

information can be obtained at www.ICGtesting.com
in the USA
1504030320
V00002B/3

7 3 4 2 7 2 4 0 6 *